Peep!

Kevin Luthardt

PEACHTREE

ATLANTA

For Alicia,
my wife and my best friend.

Thank you Jesus, my Lord and Savior.

—K. L.

Published by
PEACHTREE PUBLISHING COMPANY INC.
1700 Chattahoochee Avenue
Atlanta, Georgia 30318-2112
www.peachtree-online.com

Text and illustrations © 2003 by Kevin Luthardt

First trade paperback edition published in 2013

Illustrations created with Prismacolor colored pencils on Fabriano paper

Book design by Kevin Luthardt
Composition by Loraine M. Joyner

Printed in October 2019 at Toppan Leefung Printing Limited
10 9 8 7 6 5 4 (hardcover)
10 9 8 7 (trade paperback)

HC ISBN: 978-1-56145-046-6
PB ISBN: 978-1-56145-682-6

Library of Congress Cataloging-in-Publication Data

Luthardt, Kevin.
Peep! / by Kevin Luthardt.
p. cm.
Summary: Although a boy is lonely after the hatchling duckling that followed him home finally joins
other ducks, he soon meets another creature.
ISBN: 978-1-56145-046-6
[1. Ducks—Fiction. 2. Pets—Fiction. 3. Stories without words—Fiction.] I. Title.
PZ7.L9793 Pe 2003
[E]—dc21   2002035910

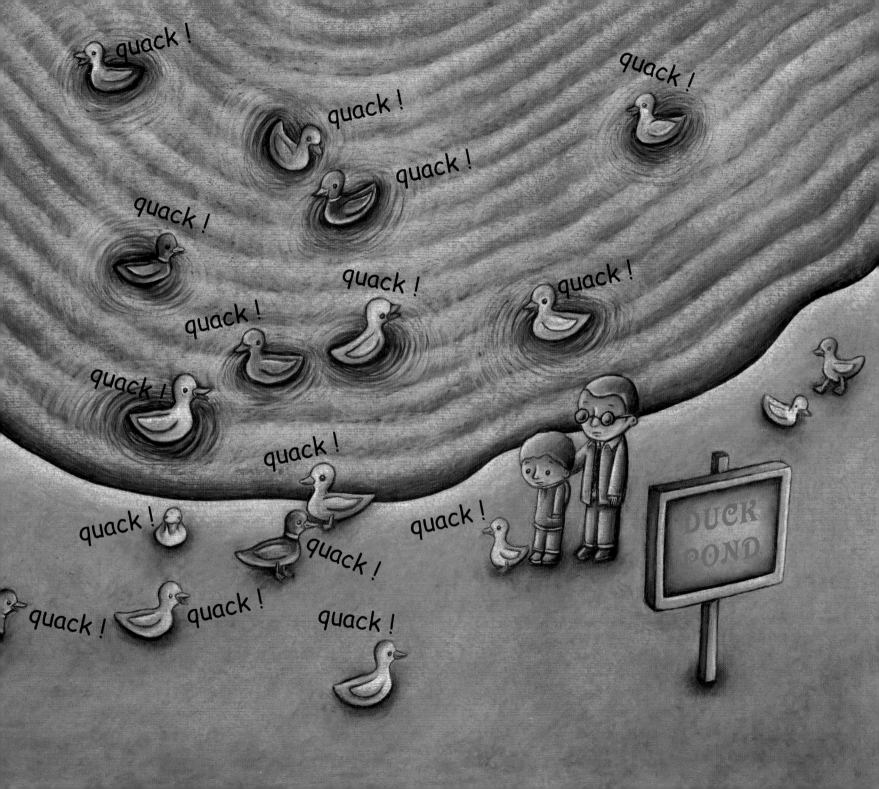

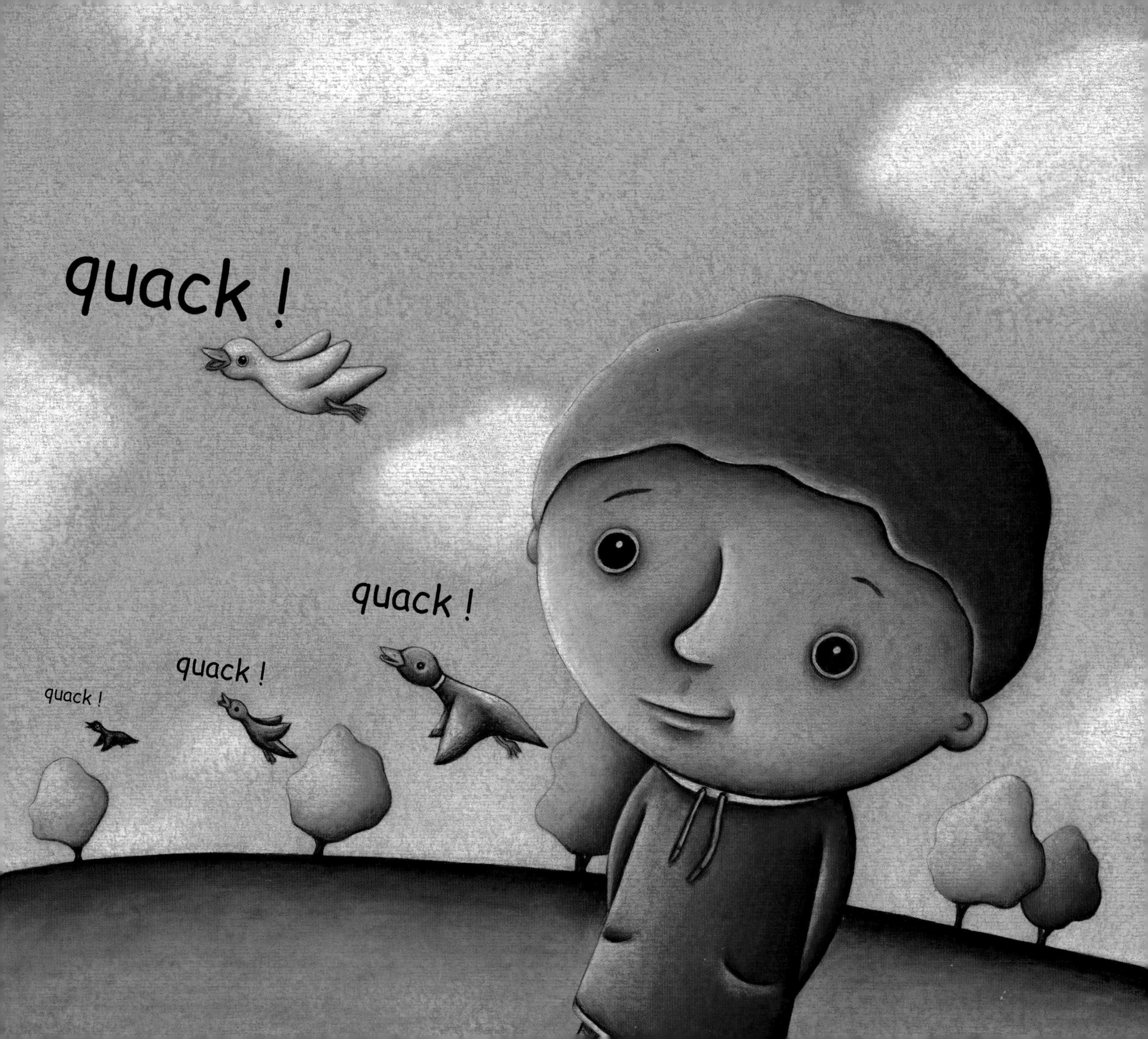
quack !
quack !
quack !
quack !